99A

THE GHOST-EYE TREE

By Bill Martin, Jr.
and John Archambault

Illustrated by
Ted Rand

Holt, Rinehart and Winston/New York

One dark and windy autumn night
when the sun had long gone down,
Mama asked my sister and me
to take the road
to the end of the town
to get a bucket of milk.

Oooo . . .
I dreaded to go . . .
I dreaded the tree. . . .
Why does Mama always choose me
when the night is so dark
and the mind runs free?

"Come on, 'fraidy cat!"
  my sister said.
"Don't hang back!"

"I'm not hangin' back,"
  I said.
"I'm getting my hat."

"Your dumb hat,"
  my sister said.
"It's too big for you.
  It makes you look stupid."

"Well, you don't have to wear it,"
  I said.

"No, but I have to look at it,"
  my sister said.

"Then look the other way,"
  I said.

Oooo . . .
how dark it was . . .
how dread it was . . .
walking the road
to the end of the town . . .
for the halfway tree . . .
the Ghost-Eye tree . . .
was feared by all . . .
the great and the small . . .
who walked the road
to the end of the town. . . .

"What's the matter now?"
 my sister said.

"My hat,"
 I said.
"It slipped off."

"You're afraid, that's what!"
 my sister said.

"I am not,"
 I said.
"I'm getting my hat."

As we neared the tree,
  our walk slowed down . . .
halfway down
  to the end of the town . . .
hiding what we feared the most . . .
pretending there would be no ghost . . .
pretending . . .
not to be . . .
afraid. . . .

"There's nothing to fear,"
  my sister said.
"There's nothing here
  but an old oak tree."

"No, there's nothing here,"
  I said.
"There's nothing to fear
  in an old oak tree."

But we ran past the tree
  as fast as we could. . . .
Nothing happened!
Nothing happened!
We felt so good
  that we started to sing,
"There's no such thing
  as a ghost!
There's no such thing
  as a ghost!"

"It's only a dream,"
  my sister said.
"It's only a fooly
  inside your head.
There's nothing to dread
  in an old oak tree."

I pulled my hat down
over one eye . . .
to look tough
like Mike Barber
in the movies.
I'm tough!
I said to myself.
Real tough!

"What?"
my sister said.

"I didn't say anything,"
I said.

"You did too!"
my sister said.
"You were muttering to yourself."

"I was not,"
I said.

"Then push up your hat,"
my sister said,
"You look stupid."

Oh,
how glad were we,
how free to be
walking the road
to the end of the town . . .
for the halfway tree,
the Ghost-Eye tree,
my sister and I
had passed it by . . .
and the road led down
to the end of the town
where we got the bucket of milk.

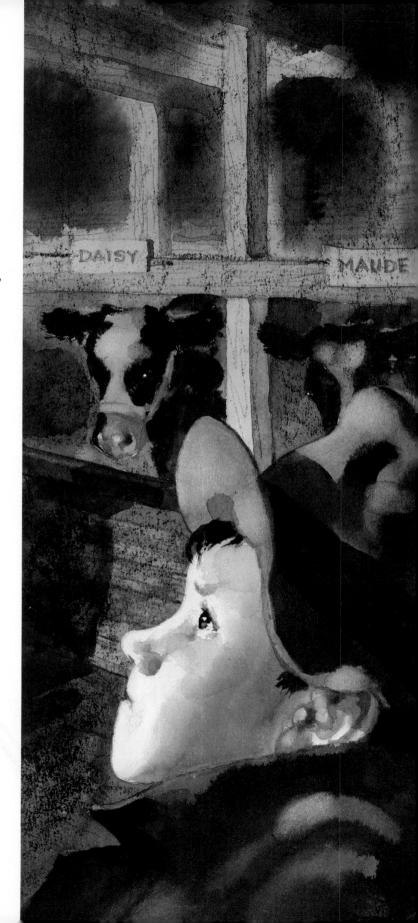

"That's a fine hat you got,"
  said Mr. Cowlander, the milkman.

I smiled.

" 'Twould make a good milk bucket,"
  said Mr. Cowlander.

My sister laughed.
I didn't.

Nobody's gonna put milk in my hat,
I said to myself.

"What?"
  said Mr. Cowlander.

"I didn't say anything,"
  I said.

"Yes, you did,"
  my sister said.
"You were muttering again.
  Mr. Cowlander,
  that hat makes him crazy.
  It's a crazy hat!"

"Well, come on,"
  I said.
"Help me carry the milk."

First, I carried . . .
then my sister carried . . .
walking home
from the end of the town . . .
we couldn't walk fast,
the milk slowed us down . . .
walking home
from the end of the town. . . .

Oooo, how dark . . .
Oooo, how dread. . . .

"Hurry up,"
  my sister said.
"We're halfway home."

"Oooo, what's that?"
  I said.

"I didn't hear anything."
  my sister said.

"But I heard . . . something . . ."
  I said.
"I really heard it . . .
  Let's go back to Mr. Cowlander's."

"No . . . no!"
  my sister said.
"There's nothing here,
  nothing to fear. . . ."

Oooo . . .
why does Mama always choose me
when the night is so dark
and the mind runs free. . . .

Oooo . . .
look . . . look . . .

The halfway tree,
the Ghost-Eye tree . . .
turned its head
and looked at me. . . .

Oooo . . .

The halfway tree . . .
the Ghost-Eye tree . . .
shook its arms . . .
and reached . . .
for ME!

eeeeo

Oh! Oooooohhhh!

We ran . . .
my sister and I . . .
Oh how we ran!
We ran . . .
all the way home . . .
as fast as we could. . . .
We set the bucket down . . .
flopped on the ground . . .
gasping . . .
for breath. . . .

"Oooo,"
  my sister said.
"I was so scared. . . ."

"Me, too,"
  I said.
"I saw the ghost. . . .
  Did you?"

"Yes,"
  my sister said.
"Don't tell Mama. . . .
  She'll worry. . . ."

"But she'll know,"
  I said.
"We spilt a lot of milk."

"That doesn't matter,"
  my sister said.
"I'll put some water in the bucket.
  She'll never know the difference.
  . . . Say! Where's your hat?"

"Oooo . . . my hat. . . .
  I lost it. . . ."
  I said.
"I lost it!"

"Where?"
  my sister said.

"Back there . . ."
  I said,
"b-b-by the Ghost-Eye tree. . . ."

"Oooo,"
  my sister said.

"But it don't matter,"
  I said.

"Yes it *does* matter,"
  my sister said.

"No,"
  I said,
"it makes me look stupid."

"It does not!"
  my sister said.
"It's a beautiful hat.
  Come on. . . .
  Let's . . .
  Let's go get it."

"No."
  I said,
"it don't matter.
  Really, it don't matter!"

Up she jumped,
   that sister of mine,
   and took to the road
   that led through the town,
   to the halfway tree,
   the Ghost-Eye tree,
   where my hat lay fallen
   on the haunted ground.

"Ellie! Ellie! Come back!"
   I cried.
"Ghost-Eye'll get you!
   He's right by your side!"

But faster than foolies
   that flash through your mind,
Ellie came back
   leaving Ghost-Eye behind.

"Here's your dumb hat,"
 my sister said.
"It makes you look stupid."

"It does not,"
 I said.
"It's a beautiful hat."

I put it on my head,
pulled it down
over one eye . . .
to look tough . . .
like Mike Barber. . . .
I'm tough!
I said to myself.
Real tough!
I ain't 'fraid
of no ghost.

But . . .
since that dread night
at the halfway tree
when Ghost-Eye tried
to frighten me,
by some lucky chance
I'm never around . . .
when Mama wants milk . . .
from the end of the town. . . .

Text copyright © 1985 by Bill Martin, Jr., and John Archambault
Illustrations copyright © 1985 by Ted Rand
All rights reserved, including the right to reproduce
this book or portions thereof in any form.
Published by Holt, Rinehart and Winston,
383 Madison Avenue, New York, New York 10017.
Published simultaneously in Canada by Holt, Rinehart
and Winston of Canada, Limited.

Library of Congress Cataloging in Publication Data
Martin, Bill, 1916–
The ghost-eye tree.
Summary: Walking down a dark lonely road on an errand
one night, a brother and sister argue over who is afraid
of the dread Ghost-Eye tree.
1. Children's stories, American. [1. Ghosts—Fiction.
2. Fear—Fiction. 3. Brothers and sisters—Fiction]
I. Archambault, John. II. Rand, Ted, ill. III. Title.
PZ7.M356773Gh 1985   [E]   85-8422

ISBN: 0-03-005632-2

First Edition

Designer: Victoria Hartman
Printed in Japan
10 9 8 7 6 5 4 3 2 1

ISBN 0-03-005632-2